This edition published in Great Britain in 2009
by Dean an imprint of Egmont UK Limited
239 Kensington High Street,
London W8 6SA
BARBIE and associated trademarks and trade dress are owned by,
and used under license from, Mattel, Inc.
© 2005, Mattel, Inc.

ISBN 978 0 6035 6448 2
1 3 5 7 9 10 8 6 4 2

Printed in Italy

$\mathcal{J}$ust over the rainbow from the world we know, lies Fairytopia. In this magical place, fairies frolic among the flowers, chasing each other and diving through the air. But one fairy is very different from the rest: Elina is the only fairy in Fairytopia without wings!

Elina can't fly, but she moves so well you would barely notice, as she chases her friend Dandelion. Elina leaps from leaf to leaf, slides down petals and swings on vines, while Dandelion soars through the air with her beautiful wings. Elina wishes she had wings, too!

Bibble, Elina's puffball, knows just what she is thinking, as Elina watches the fairies in the sky. He floats up next to her face and purrs in Elina's ear to comfort her.

At that moment, a group of pretty Pixies flutter over.

"What do you call a fairy without wings?" asks the first Pixie.

"I don't know. What?" asks the second Pixie.

"Nothing!" replies the first Pixie. "Who'd want to call a wingless fairy?!"

The Pixies laugh so hard that they turn somersaults in mid-air.

"Don't let them get to you, Elina," says Dandelion, spreading her wings to block the Pixies.

"Hey," says the first Pixie. "We came to tell you that Topaz has been kidnapped."

"Kidnapped! Oh, no!" cries Elina, looking at her friends. "Wait. Why are you telling us this?"

"Look, just because we make fun of you, that doesn't mean we want to see you kidnapped by Laverna, too," says a third Pixie.

"We're going home, where it's safe," says the first Pixie, and the Pixies fly away.

Elina and Dandelion can't believe what they've just heard. Topaz is the Guardian of Magic Meadow. Without her, the meadow isn't safe from the wicked fairy, Laverna.

Elina and Dandelion look around the meadow, nervously. All the other fairies have left, too. The flowers in the meadow are fading and their petals are beginning to droop.

"The flowers are sick," says Dandelion. "And I've noticed some fairies are having trouble flying."

Elina and Dandelion must find another Guardian Fairy who can help them. The closest Guardian Fairy is Azura, who lives all the way over in Fairy Town.

But now Dandelion is feeling the sickness, too. She is too weak to fly and she's not used to walking, so Elina and Bibble must travel to Azura's house without her.

Elina and Bibble begin their journey. They wander through parts of Fairytopia that they have never been to before, until they finally reach Fairy Town.

Far from Elina and Bibble, in the Wildering Wood, the wicked fairy, Laverna, has indeed captured Topaz. In fact, she has kidnapped all the Guardian Fairies, except Azura.

"Now, as soon as Azura arrives, you will all be together to watch me take over Fairytopia," purrs Laverna.

"You will never take over Fairytopia," says Topaz. "The fairies are loyal to the Enchantress. She's the Queen of Fairytopia."

"Oh, that's right!" says Laverna. "Why didn't I think of that? Oh wait – I did think of that!" And Laverna shows the Guardian Fairies a vat full of an odious green potion.

"At this very moment, my Firebirds are spreading this potion all over Fairytopia, causing a sickness that makes the fairies too weak to fly," explains Laverna. "And I am the only one who can help them. Not the Enchantress. All of Fairytopia will love me for it and make me their queen!"

"The Enchantress will never let you get away with it!" cries Topaz.

"Ah, the Enchantress, my dear sister," sighs Laverna.

And with that, Laverna creates a hologram of the Enchantress, which shows her lying motionless on a crystal bed.

"Oh, no!" cries Topaz.

"She's not dead, just sleeping," replies Laverna. "I slipped some of my potion in her buttercup milk. So, it looks like you will be living under my rule forever!"

Meanwhile, Elina and Bibble have arrived safely at Azura's cottage.

"Please, sit down," says Azura, leading them to a table. "You must be thirsty."

Azura claps and the flower cups are magically filled with nectar.

"Our Guardian has been kidnapped from the Magic Meadow," says Elina. "And our fairies can't fly, and the flowers are fading. I didn't know where else to go!"

Azura is horrified. There is only one thing she can do: she will go to Laverna's lair herself! But first she takes off her blue butterfly necklace, and puts it around Elina's neck.

"I want my necklace to stay safe," says Azura. "And this is a dangerous trip!"

With that, Azura flies out of the window . . . only to come face to face with Laverna's servants, the evil Funguses! She struggles against them, but it's no use. The Funguses kidnap Azura to take her to Laverna. Poor Elina watches in horror.

Now it's up to Elina to reach Laverna's lair in time to save the Guardian Fairies. But walking takes so long! Suddenly, a huge shadow falls over her. It's a giant butterfly!

"Who are you?" asks Elina.

"I'm Azura's friend, Hue," replies the giant butterfly. "I'll take you where you want to go."

Elina and Bibble hop on to Hue's back and fly high over Fairytopia, towards Laverna's lair.

"We're flying, Bibble," exclaims Elina. "We're really flying!"

After a while, they realise that they are being followed by Laverna's Firebirds. One Firebird is very close, and his jaws are wide open and his teeth bared.

"Aaaargh!!!!" they all scream together.

"Hold on, everybody!" says Hue, as he nosedives down a waterfall and zooms into a small cove.

Safely inside the cove, Elina, Hue and Bibble
meet some friendly merpeople. Prince Nalu,
a merman, explains that the Firebirds are
waiting for them just beyond the waterfall.
The only safe way out of the cove is to swim
a long way underwater.

"Eat this," says Prince Nalu, giving them some
seaweed. "It is a special type of seaweed that lets
you breathe underwater."

Hue, Elina, and Bibble don't want to eat the
sticky green seaweed, but they force some into
their mouths and then plunge into the sea.
Prince Nalu guides them through a deep sea
cavern. They are amazed that the seaweed
really works.

When they arrive at a safe place, Elina sweetly
thanks the Prince.

"I wanted to help," says Prince Nalu, taken by Elina's beauty. The two stare into each other's eyes.

"Err . . . we need to go," says Hue.

"I hope we'll meet again," says Prince Nalu, as he swims away.

Elina looks after him dreamily. Then Bibble and Elina climb aboard Hue, and they take off into the blue sky.

Meanwhile, in Laverna's lair, the Funguses deliver their prisoner, Azura, the last of the Guardian Fairies. Now Laverna can finally carry out her evil plan.

"Ah, Azura!" cries Laverna. "I was just about to explain how when I get the final necklace, I'll be able to suck the power from all the necklaces and keep it for myself."

But when Laverna looks for Azura's necklace . . . it isn't there!

"Where is your necklace?" screams
Laverna, furiously.

Azura refuses to answer, but a Fungus claims
he saw the necklace on the wingless fairy.

"Bring her to me immediately!"
commands Laverna.

Just outside the lair, Hue has caught the
sickness, so Bibble stays behind to care for him.
Elina continues alone. In no time, the Funguses
are all around her. But Elina cleverly hides
behind the giant leaves.

Elina finally makes it safely to Laverna's lair. She peeks into the throne room and discovers all the Guardian Fairies sitting in a circle, bound with ropes. Laverna is showing them the unifying crystal, which she created to absorb the power from their necklaces. The necklaces start to glow and create a rainbow of light as Laverna sucks away the fairies' power.

Suddenly, Elina runs into the room. "Let my friends go, Laverna!" she cries.

"Ahh, the wingless fairy," says Laverna. "I'll be happy to let them go if you give me Azura's necklace."

"Never!" says Elina.

Laverna flings a stream of light towards Elina and it turns into phantom wings on her back.

"I can give you wings if you join me," says Laverna.

If Elina puts the necklace around Azura's neck, the blue gem will be added to the rainbow, and then Laverna will rule Fairytopia forever!

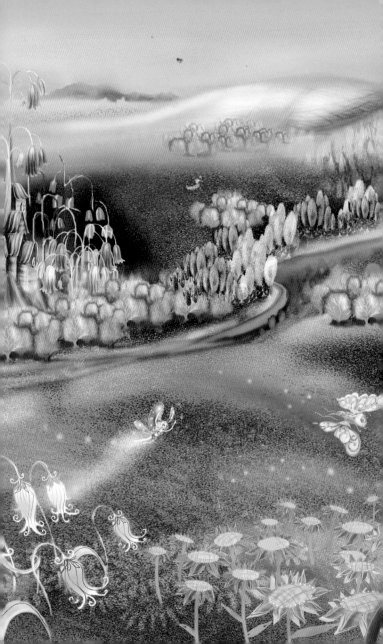

Suddenly, Elina looks hypnotized and begins to follow Laverna's orders. She removes the butterfly necklace and moves towards Azura.

"Try to wake up, Elina!" cries Azura, desperately.

But Elina doesn't listen and keeps moving forward. She lifts the necklace to place it around Azura's neck.

"Yes!" cries Laverna.

But suddenly, Elina looks up and notices the unifying crystal. She snaps out of her trance-like state and hurls Azura's necklace across the room, knocking the crystal to the floor.

"NO!!!!" cries Laverna.

The crystal shatters, and all the rainbow lights return to the fairies' necklaces. Laverna is wrapped up in a swirl of rainbow light. It begins to turn black and Laverna disappears.

The minute she is gone, the Guardian Fairies are set free, and Elina's phantom wings disappear.

Everyone is so grateful to Elina. She has saved the Guardian Fairies and Fairytopia, too!

"I knew you could do it!" cries Azura.

Suddenly, a swirl of rainbow light appears and turns into the beautiful form of the Enchantress, the Queen of Fairytopia.

"The Enchantress," gasps Hue. He bows immediately, and the others follow suit, but the Enchantress just smiles.

"I've come to thank all of you for your bravery," she says.

"Oh, thank you, but . . . we just did what we had to do," says Elina. "We weren't trying to be heroes."

"But you are," says the Enchantress. "Especially you, Elina, and I want to thank you. You have earned a great gift." And she places a butterfly necklace around Elina's neck.

"Thank you, Elina," says the Enchantress, as she disappears in a rainbow swirl.

Suddenly, the necklace glows and turns into a swirl of rainbow colours. The whirling colours turn into real wings on Elina's back! Elina looks at the wings over her shoulders, and gasps.

"I have wings!" she cries. Elina takes a deep breath and jumps into the air . . . and flies! "I'm flying!"

Everyone leaps joyfully into the air to celebrate Elina's new wings.

The Enchantress has returned Magic Meadow to health again, with all the flowers in full bloom, and the fairies laughing and playing high in the sky.

But one fairy flies especially high and laughs especially loud – Elina, a true fairy at last!

The End

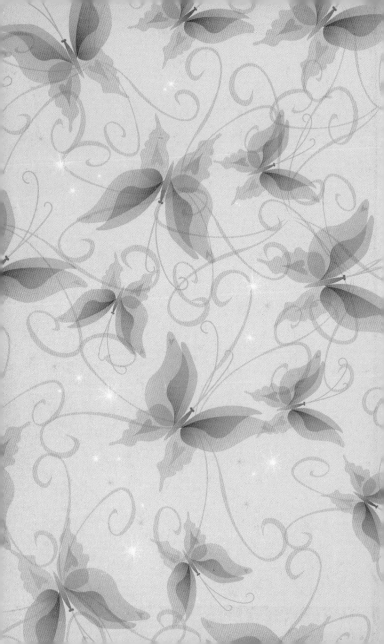